Hello Hook 'Em!

Aimee Aryal

Illustrated by Megan Craig

The University of Texas Class of 2004

MASCOT BOOKS™

www.mascotbooks.com

It was a beautiful fall day at
The University of Texas.

Hook 'Em was on his way to
Darrell K Royal – Texas Memorial Stadium
to watch a football game.

He walked by the Texas Union.

A professor passed by and waved,
"Hello Hook 'Em!"

Hook 'Em stopped by
the Littlefield Home.

A couple walking past said,
"Hello Hook 'Em!"

Hook 'Em walked over to the
Perry-Castañeda Library.

Some students standing outside said,
"Hello Hook 'Em!"

Hook 'Em stopped by the Erwin Center
where the Longhorns play basketball.

A group of Texas fans standing nearby waved, "Hello Hook 'Em!"

It was almost time for the football game.
As Hook 'Em walked to the stadium,
he passed by some alumni.

The alumni remembered Hook 'Em from when they went to UT. They said, "Hello, again, Hook 'Em!"

Finally, Hook 'Em arrived at
Darrell K Royal – Texas Memorial Stadium.

As he ran onto the football field
with Bevo, the crowd signaled,
"Hook 'Em Horns!"

Hook 'Em watched the game from the
sidelines and cheered for the team.

The Longhorns scored six points!
The quarterback shouted,
"Touchdown Hook 'Em!"

At half-time the Longhorn Band
performed on the field.

Hook 'Em and the crowd sang,
"Texas Fight."

The Texas Longhorns won
the football game!

Hook 'Em gave Coach Brown
a high-five. The coach said,
"Great game Hook 'Em!"

After the football game, Hook 'Em
was tired. It had been a long day
at The University of Texas.

He walked home and climbed into bed.
"Goodnight Hook 'Em."

For Anna and Maya, and all of
Hook 'Em's little fans. ~ AA

For my father, Allan, my mother, Claire, and for Matt.
Thank you for all of your love and support. ~ MC

Special thanks to:

Mack Brown

Craig Westemeier

For information please contact Mascot Books,
P.O. Box 220157, Chantilly, VA 20153-0157.

THE UNIVERSITY OF TEXAS, TEXAS, LONGHORNS, UT, HOOK 'EM HORNS,
BEVO, HORNS are registered trademarks of The University of Texas
and are used under license.

ISBN: 1-932888-10-1

Printed in the United States.

www.mascotbooks.com